Baby Drago

Big Sneeze

Written by
Sheryl Bass

Illustrated by
Remesh Ram

Acknowledgements

Just like it takes a village to help a sick dragon, it took a village to create this book. I would like to thank April Cox, my Yoda on this publishing journey and Remesh Ram, who masterfully created such vivid and delighful illustrations. I also would like to thank my mom, Iris Bass, my sister, Aviva Bass, my nephews, Rafi and Angelo and my loving husband, Neil Cline, who all painstakingly evaluated each text iteration, illustration, and logo submission.

Publisher's Cataloging-in-Publication data

Names: Bass, Sheryl, author. | Ram, Remesh, illustrator.
Title: Baby dragon's big sneeze / by Sheryl Bass; illustrated by Remesh Ram.
Description: McHenry, IL: Be-Kind Publishing, 2022. | Summary: When a young dragon accidentally burns down a village with a fiery sneeze, the townspeople are angry until a brave little girl enters his cave and learns that the poor dragon is sick.
Identifiers: LCCN: 2022918064 | ISBN: 979-8-9870406-1-4 (hardcover) | 979-8-9870406-0-7 (paperback) | 979-8-9870406-2-1 (ebook)
Subjects: LCSH Dragons--Juvenile fiction. | Kindness--Juvenile fiction. | Friendship--Juvenile fiction. | BISAC JUVENILE FICTION / General | JUVENILE FICTION / Animals / Dragons, Unicorns & Mythical | JUVENILE FICTION / Fairy Tales & Folklore / General | JUVENILE FICTION / Social Themes / Emotions & Feelings | JUVENILE FICTION / Social Themes / Friendship
Classification: LCC PZ7.1.B374 Ba 2022 | DDC [E]--dc23

Dedication

I would like to dedicate this book to my father, Hal Bass, who was always my biggest champion, but who passed away before he could view the beautiful illustrations in color.

I will tell you a story from legends of old,
of a huge baby dragon who caught a bad cold.

He had soared through the villages just as he pleased,
until one autumn day, he regrettably sneezed.

Fire burst from his mouth and
it burned every shack,
so the townspeople planned
a great dragon attack.

When he saw what he did,
the young dragon got scared,
and wrote an apology note
that declared:

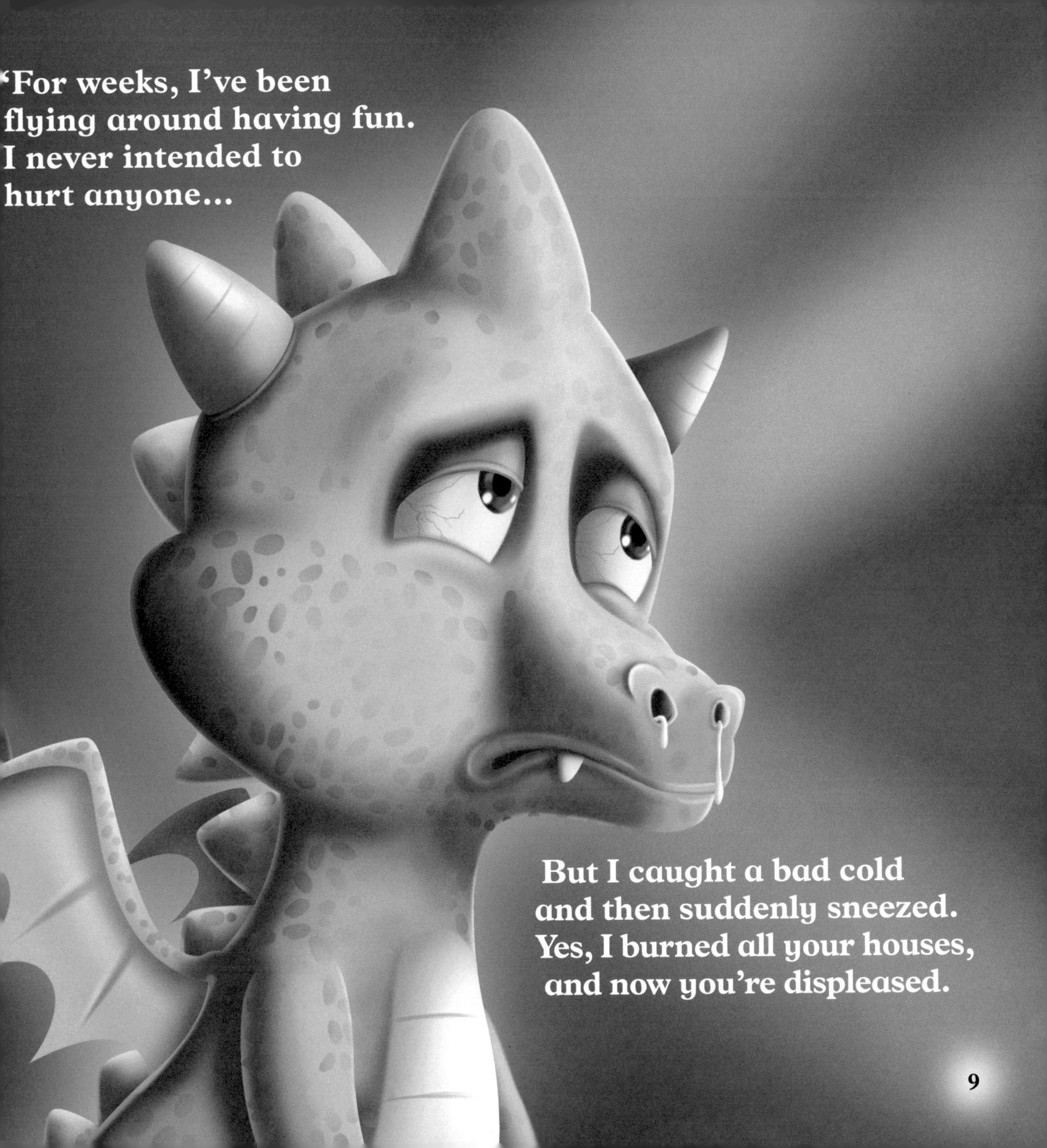

'For weeks, I've been
flying around having fun.
I never intended to
hurt anyone...

But I caught a bad cold
and then suddenly sneezed.
Yes, I burned all your houses,
and now you're displeased.

If someone could help me to finally mend,
I'd love to assist you and be your new friend."

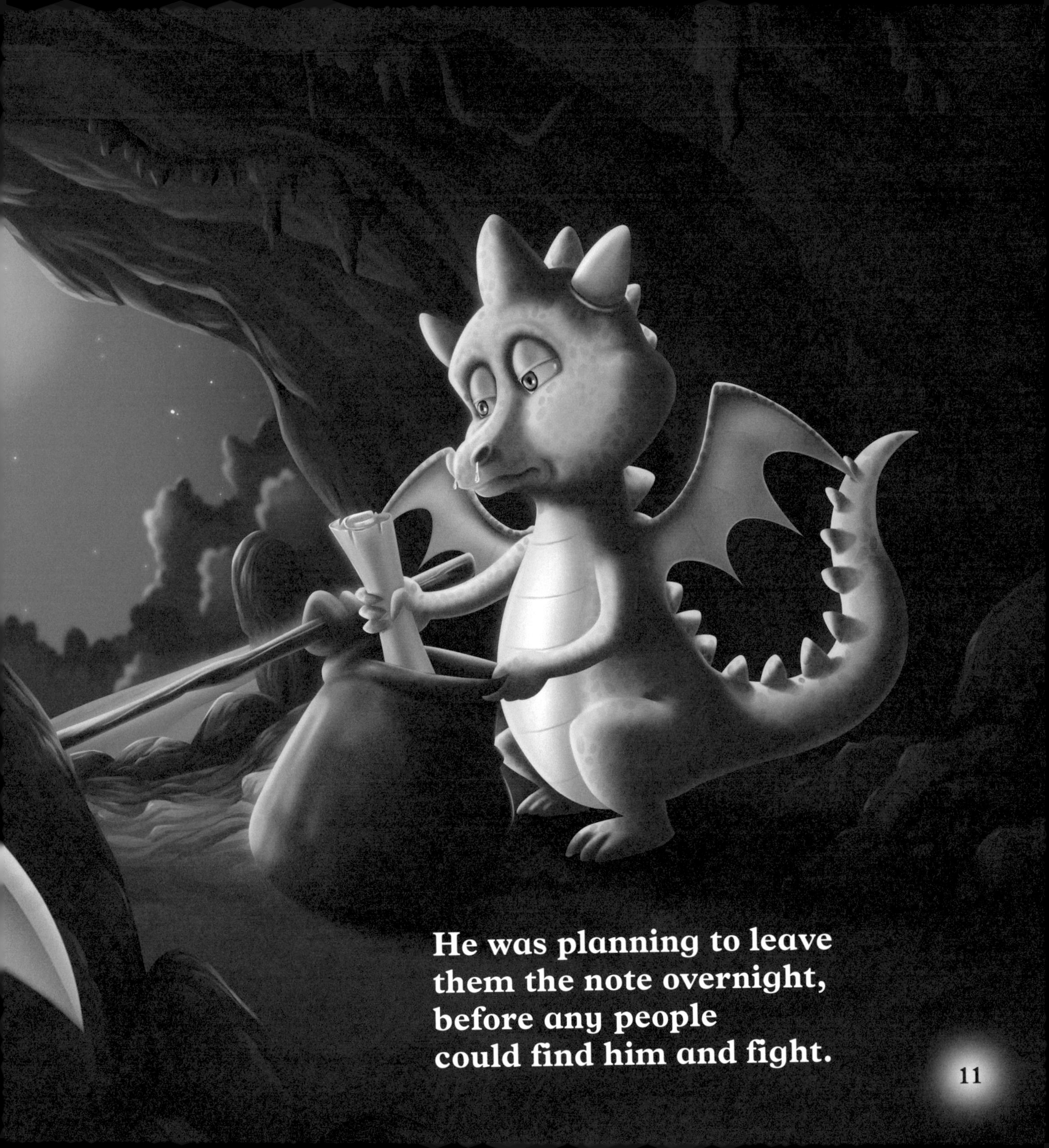

He was planning to leave
them the note overnight,
before any people
could find him and fight.

But then Mirabelle came
to his cavern to learn
why the dragon would suddenly
make their homes burn.

She steeled up her courage
and entered his cave.
"Dear dragon," she asked him,
"why won't you behave?"

“I can’t help it,” he told her.
“I’m terribly sick.
I need fireproof tissues
and medicine quick!”

She frowned with confusion.
"You sound pretty bad.
Perhaps get some help from your
mom or your dad."

He said he had hatched
all alone in this den,
and then sneezed—
but he'd try not to do it again!

Then Mirabelle said,
"I'll go talk to the king,
but until then, please cover
your mouth with your wing!"

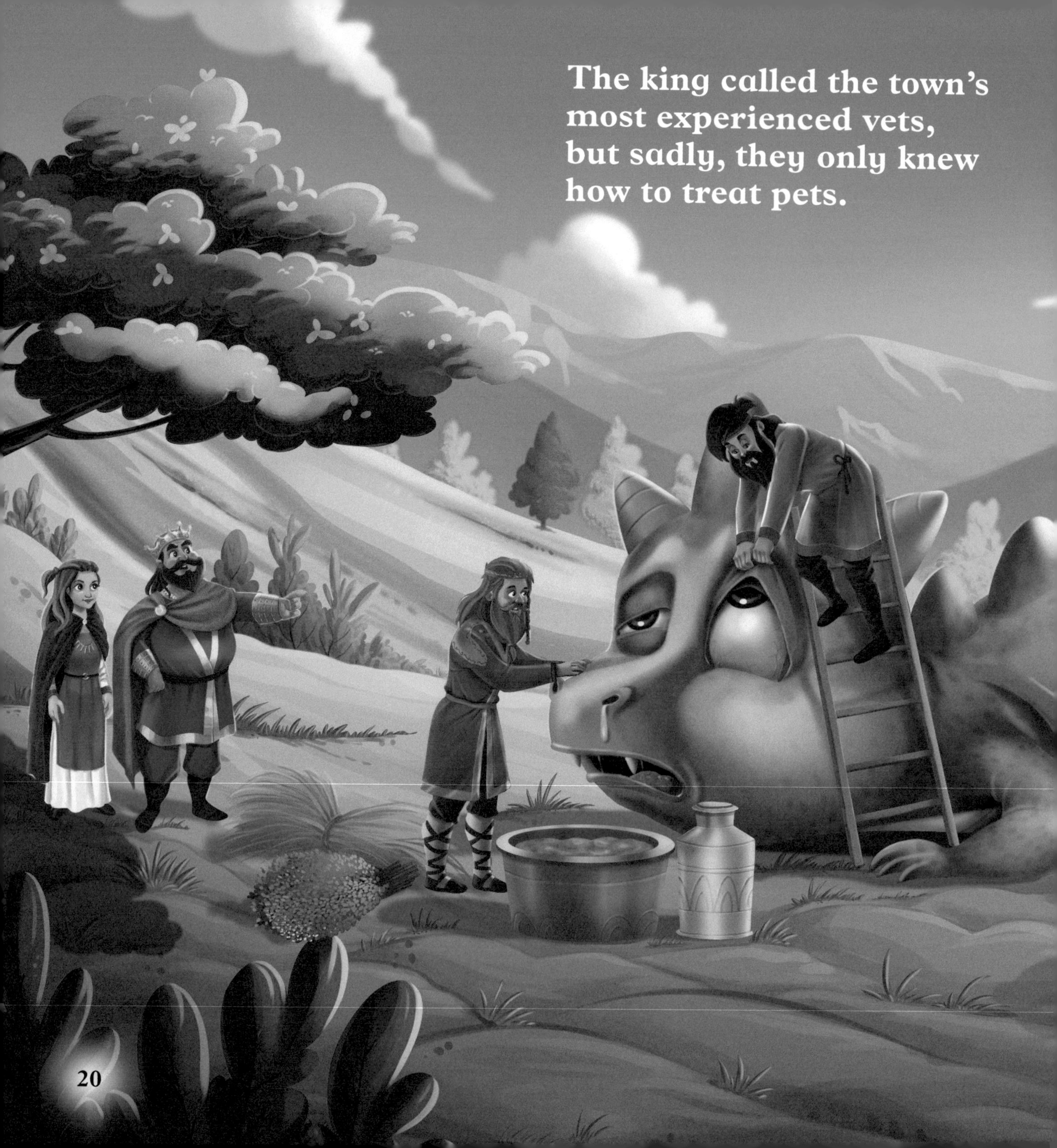

The king called the town's most experienced vets, but sadly, they only knew how to treat pets.

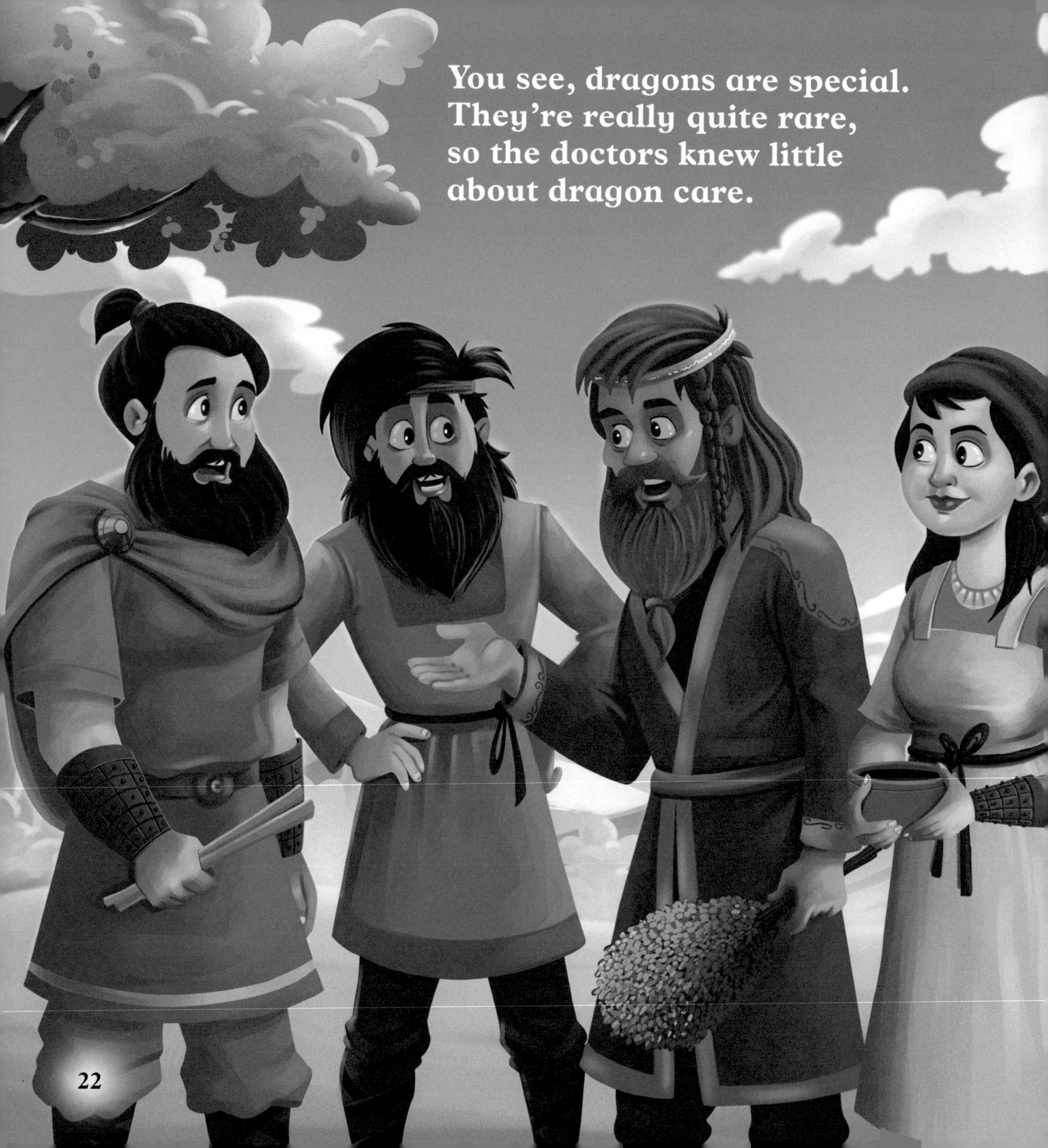

You see, dragons are special.
They're really quite rare,
so the doctors knew little
about dragon care.

But the once-angry people
could now comprehend,
that the big, lonely dragon
just needed a friend.

Some kind parents took care to
arrange his great nest,
so the dragon could bed down
for much-needed rest.

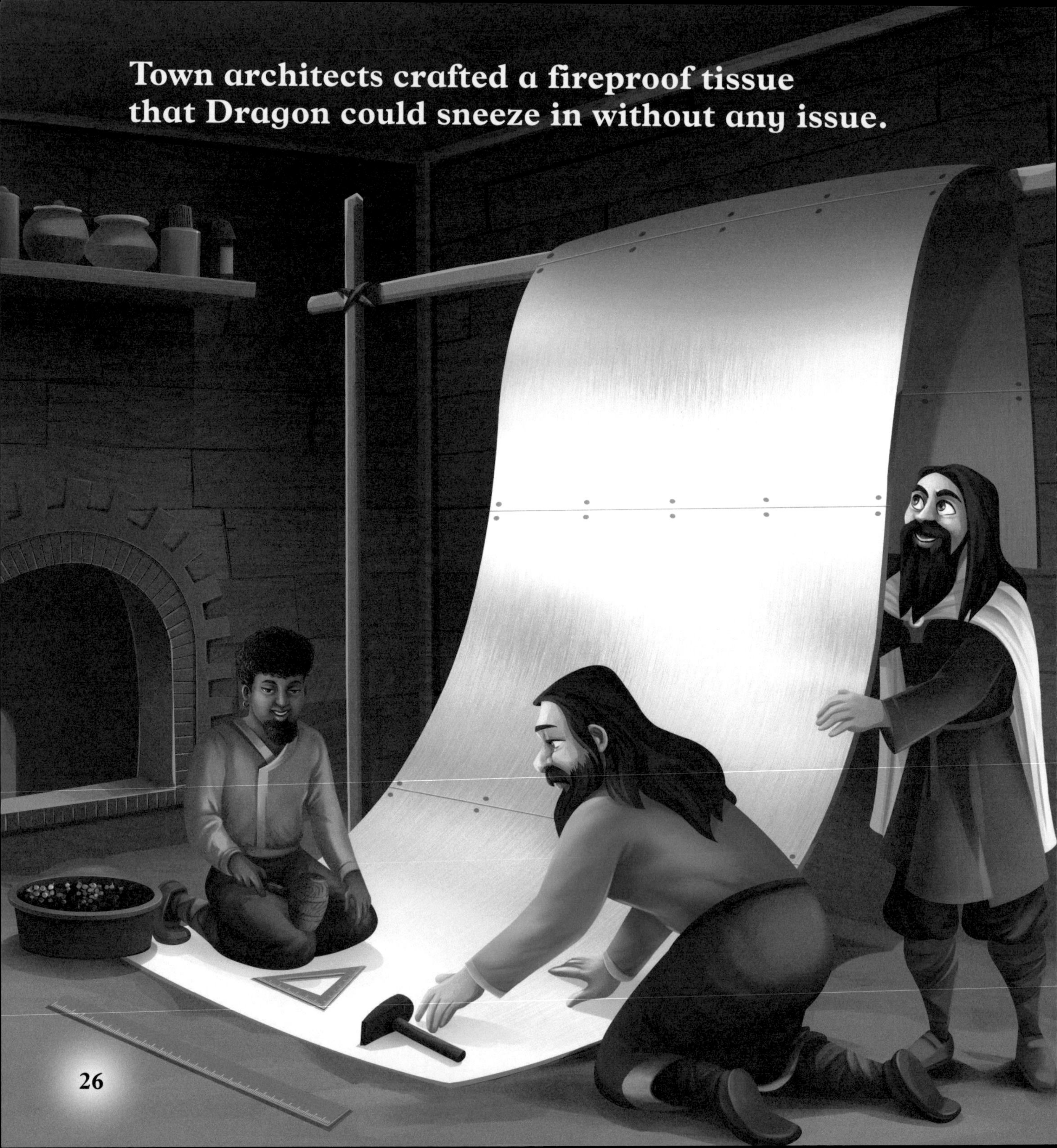

Town architects crafted a fireproof tissue
that Dragon could sneeze in without any issue.

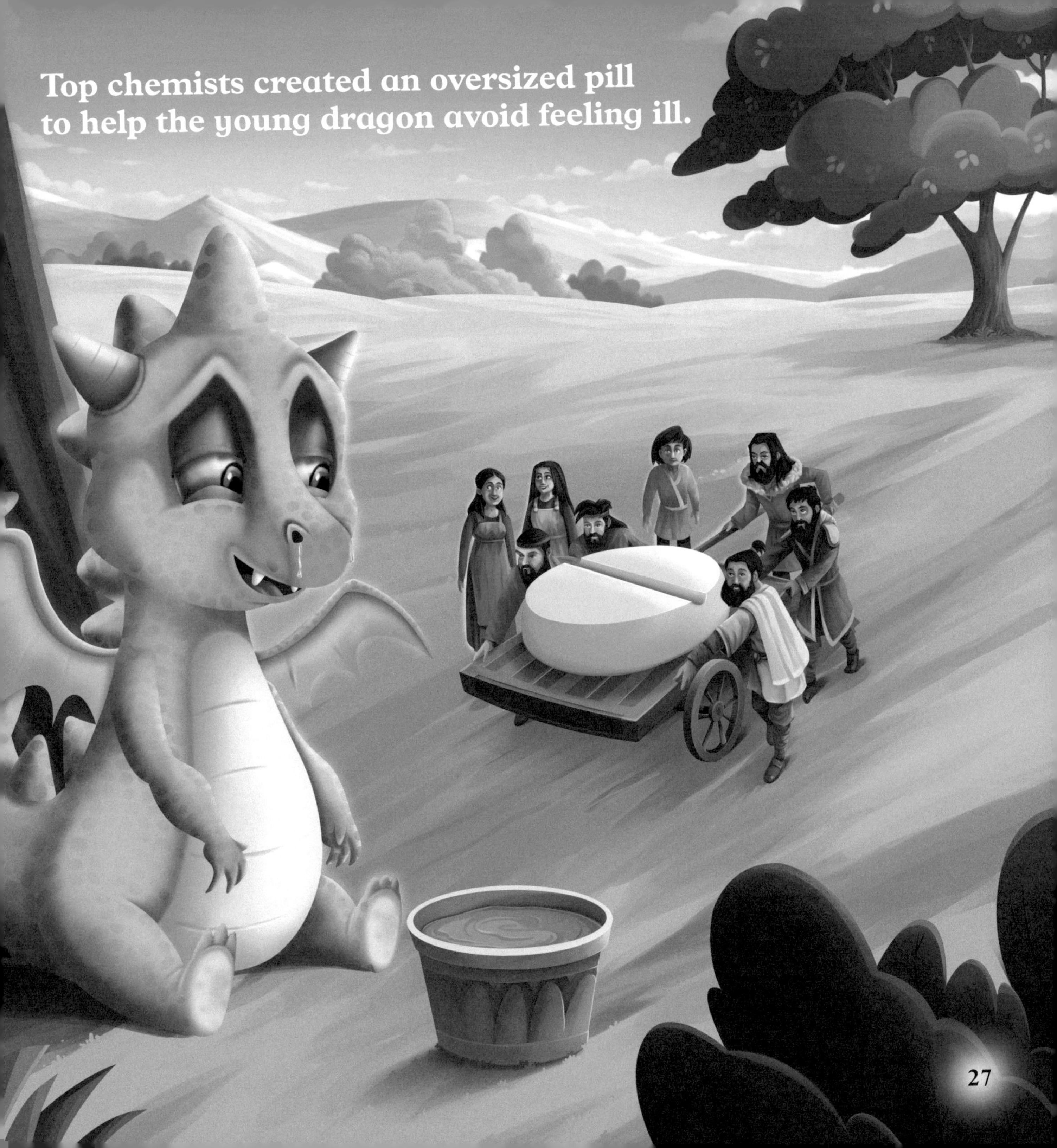

Top chemists created an oversized pill
to help the young dragon avoid feeling ill.

They made enough soup
for a neighborhood feast,
but the bowl was just right
for this towering beast.

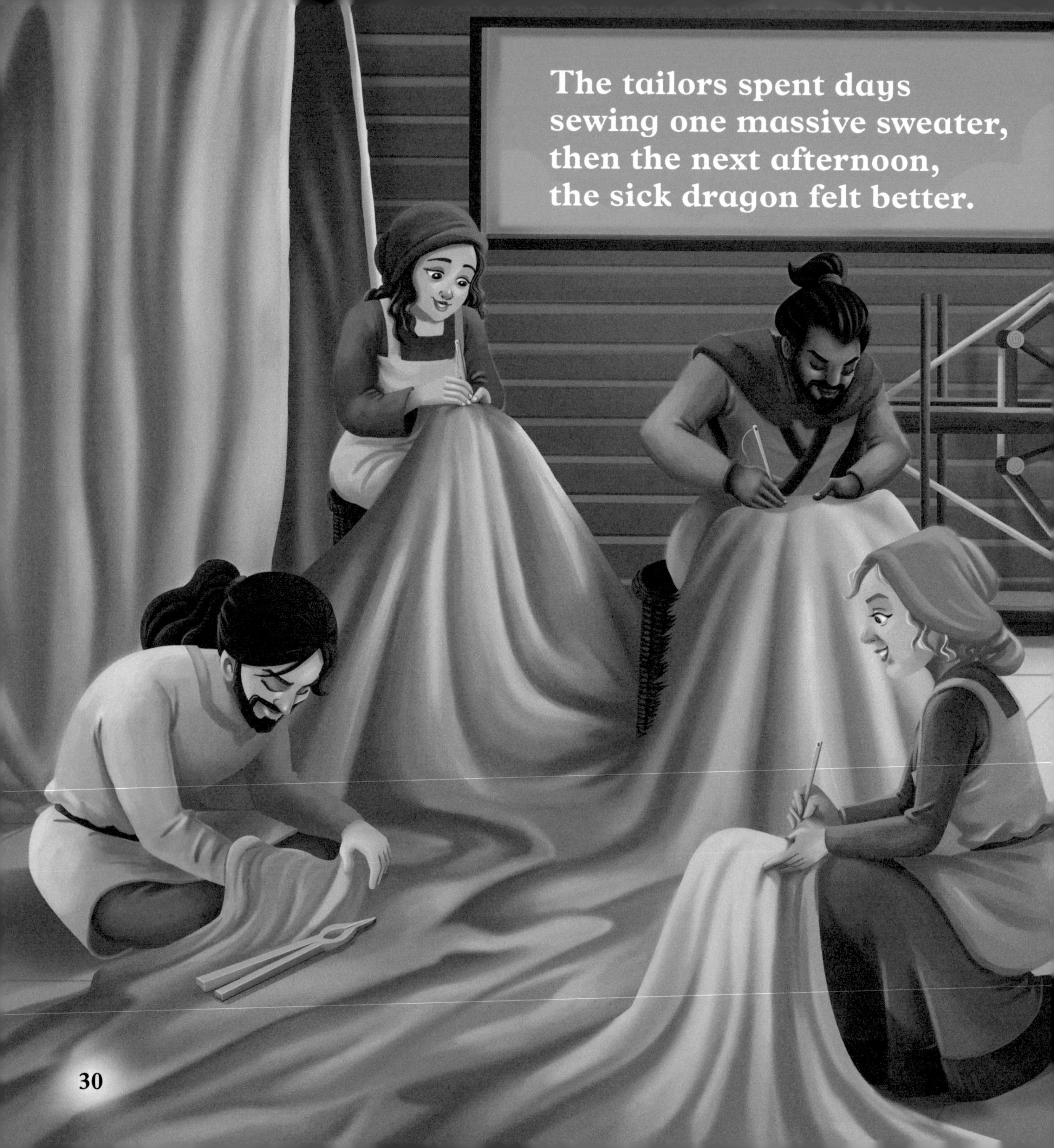

The tailors spent days
sewing one massive sweater,
then the next afternoon,
the sick dragon felt better.

"Oh, thank you so much,"
the young dragon declared.
"I am really quite honored
to know you all cared."

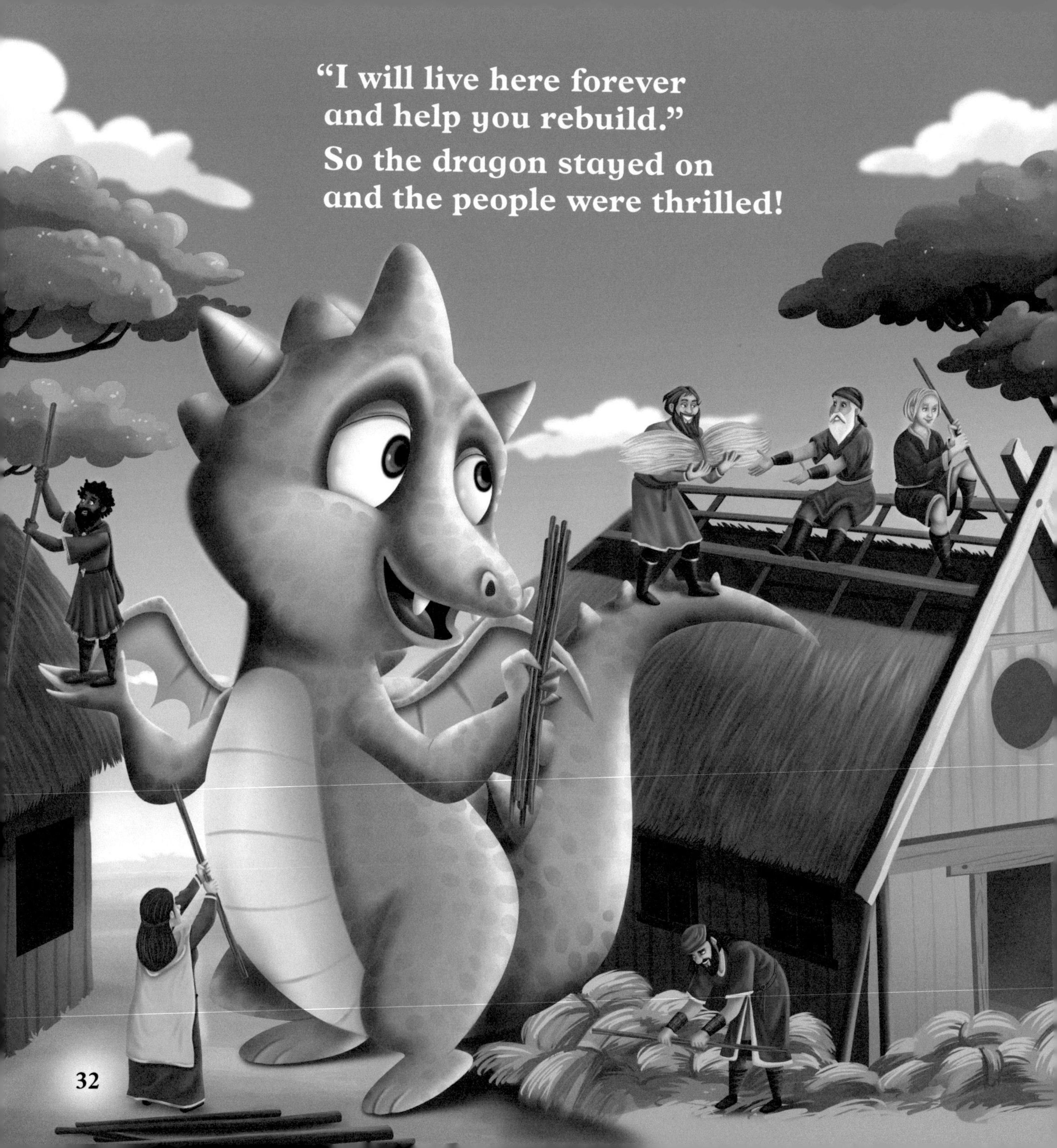

"I will live here forever
and help you rebuild."
So the dragon stayed on
and the people were thrilled!

The End

About the Author

SHERYL BASS, M.A., M.S.W., holds a master's degree in Social Work, and has studied child development. She uses these insights to inform her picture book writing. Sheryl also holds a master's degree in Journalism, and is currently working in public relations. Her goal is to produce lighthearted rhyming stories with gentle themes of teamwork and friendship. Sheryl resides just outside of Chicago, IL with her husband and two terriers.

www.be-kindpublishing.com

We hope you enjoyed this book.

Go to be-kindpublishing.com where you can download coloring pages.

It would mean the world to us if you left a review. Scan the QR code or visit the link.

https://bit.ly/Dragon-Review

If you enjoyed this book,
be sure to purchase the sequel,
Baby Dragon Finds His Family

Made in the USA
Columbia, SC
25 October 2024